Cupid and Psyche

pictures by Ati Forberg

CUPID AND PSYCHE

A Love Story

retold by EDNA BARTH

Clarion Books

TICKNOR & FIELDS : A HOUGHTON MIFFLIN COMPANY

New York

Note

Psyche is pronounced si'-ke.

Second Printing

Clarion Books
Ticknor & Fields, a Houghton Mifflin Company

Library of Congress Cataloging in Publication Data

Barth, Edna.   Cupid and Psyche.
"A Clarion book."
SUMMARY: The Greek god of love, Cupid, falls in love
with the beautiful mortal, Psyche.
1. Cupid—Juvenile literature. 2. Psyche (Goddess)—
Juvenile literature. [1. Cupid. 2. Psyche (Goddess)
3. Mythology, Greek] I. Forberg, Ati. II. Title.
PZ8.1.B3Cu   [292]   76-8821   ISBN 0-395-28840-1
(Previously published by The Seabury Press
under ISBN 0-8164-3174-4.)

Cupid and Psyche

In ancient times there lived a king and queen who had three daughters. All agreed that the two elder daughters were very beautiful. As for the third, she was so beautiful that people came from all over the kingdom just to gaze at her. Her name was Psyche.

Crowds waited at the palace gates for hours on the chance that Psyche might step into the garden. When she did appear, her incredible beauty sent a hush over the waiting throng.

"Like a goddess," one and all declared in low, awestruck tones. Then, touched by Psyche's youth and innocence, they usually added, "a very young goddess."

Another head might have been turned by all this attention. Not Psyche's. Indeed, it was astonishing how modest and sweet-natured she remained. If the young princess had any shortcomings, it was hard to discover them.

True, she was inclined to be somewhat too curious. From time to time she would begin to muse over where she might be a year or even five or ten years hence. And now and then she was heard to remark, "I do wonder what my future husband will look like."

Of course this was none of her concern at all. This was something for her father, the King, to decide. But no one is perfect, not even a princess.

Meanwhile, with each passing day, Psyche became, if anything, even lovelier. Word of her beauty spread far beyond her father's kingdom, and people journeyed over land and sea in order to gaze at her.

"Is it possible that Venus, the goddess of love and beauty, has come to earth to live among us?" some of them asked.

"Anything the gods will is possible," others replied. "But more likely the earth has borne a new Venus, all the lovelier for being young and innocent."

Few any longer visited the shrines sacred to the true goddess of love. The rites and festivals that had once been held in Venus' honor were forgotten. Her temples were falling into ruins.

The homage Venus had once received was now being showered upon Psyche. Wherever the princess walked she was followed by adoring throngs. They blew kisses to her and presented her with garlands of roses, the flowers that were sacred to Venus. Feasts were held in Psyche's honor, and sacrifices offered up in her name.

The King and Queen reveled in their daughter's glory. Psyche herself, still curiously unspoiled, simply accepted it. But Psyche's sisters were both jealous.

"What right has she, the youngest, to such attention?" complained the next to eldest sister. "It's unfitting."

"It is unfitting," agreed the eldest, "and unjust as well. Something should be done about it. It's clear that our parents will do nothing. You and I may have to take matters into our own hands."

But soon afterward, first one sister and then the other married and went to live in a distant kingdom.

Her sisters were not alone in being jealous of Psyche. Venus, too, had found out what was going on and was quite beside herself. "What an outrage!" she cried, storming through her marble halls on Mount Olympus.

Jupiter, the King of the Gods, had pronounced Venus more beautiful even than his wife Juno, Queen of Heaven. Was a lowly mortal to share her glory? "Never!" declared Venus, and she made up her mind to destroy Psyche.

"Summon Cupid," Venus ordered Mercury, the messenger of gods and goddesses. "It's time that unruly son of mine gave up his carefree ways and became useful."

Nonetheless, when Cupid stood before her, his quiver nearly empty of arrows, Venus smiled in spite of herself. Her son's golden hair was tousled. His cheeks were flushed. His eyes danced with mischief and good humor.

Cupid's chief delight was in flying about with his bow and a quiver of arrows designed not to kill but to arouse passion. And what mischief he performed, tearing one loving couple apart, mismatching another, breaking up marriages of many years! No one was safe from him, not even his mother, for Cupid made no exception of gods and goddesses.

Although fully grown, the young god still lived the life of a spoiled child. Something really should be done about it, Venus thought. But just now her main concern was her rival Psyche. So, telling Cupid what had happened, she said, "If you have even a scrap of love or respect for your mother, you will punish this detestable girl. Think of the many hearts you have played havoc with, even mine. Use your arrows to good purpose for once. See that this wretched Psyche falls in love with some vile monster."

11

His eyes bright at the prospect of such mischief, Cupid agreed. In his mother's garden were two fountains, one of sweet water and one of bitter. Filling small, amber vials with some of each, Cupid hung them on his quiver. After sunset he spread his wings and flew through the night toward the city where Psyche's parents had their palace. Shortly before dawn, he reached the chamber where Psyche lay sleeping.

Like all who gazed at her, Cupid was struck by Psyche's beauty and her look of innocence. For a moment, something like pity stirred in him. But, remembering his mother's orders, he let a few drops from the bitter fountain spill over Psyche's lips. Then he touched her side with the tip of his arrow.

Psyche's large, wondering eyes opened but she could see no one, for Cupid had taken care to remain invisible.

However, Cupid could see Psyche. Indeed her wide-eyed beauty so startled him that he pricked himself with his own arrow.

At once his heart filled with love for Psyche, and with the

love came regret for having harmed her. To think of having sprinkled such a lovely creature with the bitter drops that could cause her to love a monster!

In order to undo the mischief, Cupid quickly emptied the vial of sweet water over Psyche's hair. Then, helplessly in love, he departed.

As time passed, Psyche took less and less pleasure in her beauty. She thought often of her two sisters. All agreed that their beauty could not compare with hers, yet both had long since been married to kings. Psyche herself might as well have been an exquisite statue. Young men came by the thousands to gaze at her but not one ever asked for her hand. They were too much in awe of her.

"Beauty like mine is a curse," Psyche thought at times. "I'd be better off if I'd been born plain."

There were times, too, when she wished she'd been born a prince instead of a princess. A prince could look forward to doing brave deeds or to ruling a kingdom. For a princess there was nothing in store but marriage. And Psyche could not even look forward to that. Or so it appeared.

As year after year went by, Psyche's father became alarmed. A king with an unwed daughter was quite unheard of! Psyche should long since have been married to someone of royal or noble birth. But no man of suitable rank had so much as proposed. What could be lacking in Psyche?

Certainly not beauty. The whole kingdom, indeed the whole world, could testify to Psyche's beauty.

The King grew thoughtful. Suppose that was the very trouble. By allowing his daughter to be worshipped like some beautiful goddess, suppose he had angered the gods?

On the Queen's advice, Psyche's father made preparations for a visit to the Temple of Apollo at Miletus, a journey of twelve days. There, with a sense of foreboding, he consulted the oracle. "Where shall I find a husband for my beautiful daughter whom no man wishes to marry?"

The answer of the oracle made him tremble:

> Dress your daughter in deepest mourning
> and lead her up to some lonely peak,
> there to await her bridegroom.
> Let her expect no mortal.
> Her husband-to-be is a winged monster,
> one that even the gods fear.

When the King returned with the dreadful news, the whole kingdom went into mourning. For days, the royal couple shut themselves within the palace, brooding and weeping. Only Psyche herself remained unmoved. For what-

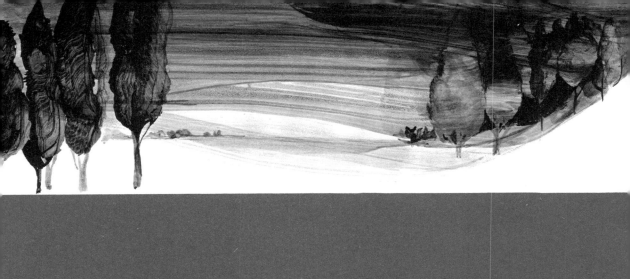

ever her future, it could be no worse than the dreary present.

The King and Queen delayed the journey for as long as they dared. But, in time, arrangements were made for the marriage the gods had willed.

The hour came and the procession formed. The torches burned with low, melancholy flames. Instead of a wedding march, the flutes piped a soft lament. The bride was dressed as if for a funeral.

Slowly, followed by grieving throngs, the bridal procession moved off toward the mountain. At the head, like one going to her grave, walked Psyche, her eyes dry and her face like marble.

The weeping King and Queen tried once to halt the procession, but Psyche stopped them. "Your tears come too late," she said dully. "You should have wept for me when your subjects first hailed me as the new Venus. From that moment on I was doomed and the same as dead."

Psyche's words sent a chill through the hearts of her parents for they knew that she spoke the truth. On the mountaintop they sadly bade her a last farewell. Then, followed by their dejected subjects, they turned homeward.

From the lonely summit, Psyche watched the procession disappear. Then the tears she had been holding back began falling. Soon, relieved by her weeping, she thought about the past few years.

Her life from now on would at least be different. A winged monster for a husband! She knew she ought to be filled with dread. Instead, she was becoming curious.

Psyche waited and waited, but no one at all appeared. Finally Zephyr, the kindly west wind, began blowing gently around her. Psyche's robes filled with air and she felt herself being lightly lifted, then floating downward into a valley.

There she was lowered onto a bed of softest grass. The air was soft, too, and filled with the fragrance of flowers. Soothed by the peace and beauty all around her, Psyche fell fast asleep.

When she awoke it was still daylight. Rested and strangely calm, Psyche rose and walked toward a grove of stately trees that stood beckoning to her.

Within the grove was a stream of clear water that led her onward to a large clearing, where she stopped and gave a gasp. Before her was a palace so splendid that Psyche's first thought was that some god must be in residence there. Built of pure white marble, it rose serene amid green gardens abloom with white flowers.

The palace gates stood open as if in welcome. So, without hesitating, Psyche stepped into the courtyard and up to the door.

Rather than grandeur, the anterooms and the halls of the palace had a kind of radiance. Instead of solemnity, there was a light, joyful feeling everywhere.

Beyond the lovely halls were chamber after chamber filled with treasure. Most amazing of all, there was not a chain, bolt or lock anywhere, or a single sign of any occupant.

As Psyche stood gazing about in awe and wonder, a voice from nowhere began speaking. "All that you see is yours. The door at the right leads to your bedchamber. Rest there as long as you like. When you go to your bath, we will attend you. After that you will enjoy your wedding banquet. I am one of your many servants."

Psyche did as the invisible maid suggested. She went to her chamber, and there on a bed soft as air, she rested.

After her nap, Psyche enjoyed a bath in a pool fed with waters that not only cleansed her but also soothed her. Gentle, invisible hands dried her and sprinkled her with fragrant oils. Then the unseen attendants dressed her in a

gown of spun silk, a veil of the lightest gossamer, and slippers made of rose petals. In her hands they placed a bouquet of small, pearl-like flowers.

She was led into a splendid hall and up to a table that was laid for a banquet. The moment she took her seat, delicious dishes appeared from nowhere. The waiters were only voices but they seemed to know, without being told, exactly what Psyche wanted. The tender meats and tasty sauces, the delicate greens, the mellow cheeses, the juicy grapes, figs, and pomegranates, and the sweets that followed were truly ambrosial. The wines were like nectar.

When asked by the chief waiter if the banquet was satisfactory, Psyche replied, "It is more than that. This is a feast fit for a god or goddess."

For entertainment there were solos by unseen musicians, and these were followed by bursts of song from an invisible choir.

With all this there was no sign of any bridegroom, so when the time came, Psyche thanked the voices and retired to her chamber.

During the night, she awoke to find someone beside her, murmuring to her.

"My monster husband!" thought Psyche with a start. Then as she felt the strong, gentle arms and heard the loving tones of her husband's voice, any fear that she had vanished. Without being told, she knew that her husband was no monster. Instead, he was the essence of love itself.

"I love you with all my heart, Psyche," her husband told her, "and I always shall, but on one condition. You will never be able to see me. If you even attempt to, all will be over."

Puzzled as she was, Psyche decided that this was no stranger than anything else that had happened since she and her parents had parted.

When morning came, her husband was gone, but she was told that he would be back that evening. With all the voices to keep her company, she waited contentedly for his return.

Several weeks went by like this. But the day came when Psyche gave in to her weakness of wanting to know too much. "I do wonder what my husband looks like," she said to herself. "Like a god, I daresay, if he is as handsome as he is loving."

That evening she kissed her husband and begged, "For

once, my love, stay until daylight. I so long to see your face."

Her husband refused. "If you loved me as I love you, what I look like would be unimportant," he chided. His arms tightened about her, and he asked softly, "Aren't you happy with me? Would you rather I were someone else?"

"No! No!" protested Psyche. "I wouldn't exchange you for Cupid himself!"

Loving and loved in return, and surrounded by every comfort, Psyche was contented for a time. Then, as the wonder of it faded, she grew bored with the long, idle days and the people she could talk with but never see.

More and more often her thoughts turned to her parents and sisters. How sad they must be, thinking her as good as dead. If only they could hear about her good fortune.

One evening she told her husband of her longing. "Let my sisters come to visit me," she pleaded. "Let them rejoice with me in my happiness and take news of me to my parents."

"No, indeed!" declared her husband. "Your sisters are not what you think, Psyche, and you must promise never to see them. Give me your word of honor."

Psyche gave her word, but by morning she regretted it. As usual, her husband had gone, and here she was in what was really nothing more than a splendid prison, with only the tiresome voices to keep her company. "Oh, I can't bear it!" cried Psyche. Her sobs echoed through the vast rooms of the lonely palace.

When her husband returned that evening, Psyche was still sobbing. Nothing he said was of any comfort. "You are my husband," she said, "but I am never allowed to see you. At least let me see my sisters, if only for a short visit. Otherwise I shall die of sorrow."

"Very well," he agreed at last. "See them if you must, but remember—you may come to regret it."

Overjoyed at the thought of being with her sisters again, Psyche scarcely heard his warning. At dawn the next day, she summoned Zephyr and gave him her husband's orders. Then the gentle west wind wafted Psyche's sisters to the palace.

They were both much astonished to see her for they had long thought their sister dead. "Little Psyche!" they cried, embracing her, "how well you look!"

"Come along now," said Psyche after she had asked about her parents and her sisters' husbands. Happily she led her sisters through the palace. She showered them with precious necklaces, bracelets, rings, and brooches to take home as keepsakes. She ordered baths for them, and served them a banquet at her magical table.

Seeing no servants, and hearing all the voices, Psyche's sisters exchanged glances. What a strange palace their sister lived in, but in what luxury! Their own way of life was nothing compared with this, and they were both nearly sick with envy.

With a false smile on her face, the older one asked, "Who is the husband who surrounds you with such splendor, sister? If he is as handsome as he is wealthy, I daresay he looks like a god."

"Oh, he does," said Psyche quickly. "Like a young god."

Psyche's sisters were both married to elderly kings so this made them even more envious. "When are we to meet him?" they asked.

"Oh, what a pity," said Psyche, quickly making up another story. "I'm afraid you won't meet him. You see, he spends his days hunting in the hills and valleys near here."

"What is your husband's name?" the sisters demanded. "How tall is he? What color are his eyes? Is he dark or fair?"

No matter how often Psyche changed the subject they always returned to it. At last she broke down and confessed that she had never had so much as a glimpse of her own husband.

Her sisters stared at her in astonishment. Then they burst into scornful laughter. "An invisible husband!" scoffed the younger one. "Who ever heard of that?"

"Take my advice," said the older one darkly. "Find out what he looks like, Psyche. You were destined to marry a monster, you know. Why do you think he feeds you these delicacies? Probably because he plans to devour you."

Psyche had long since forgotten what the oracle had told her father, but she remembered it now, and shuddered.

Seeing her weaken, the older sister went on, "Do as I tell you, Psyche. Hide a small lamp and a sharp carving knife in your chamber. When your husband is fast asleep, light the lamp and see what he looks like. If he is the monster that I suspect he is, cut off his head."

"Only then will you be safe from him," added the younger sister.

After her sisters left, Psyche could think of nothing else. Suppose they were right, and her husband really was a vicious monster? If this was so, it was no wonder that he had forbidden her ever to look at him!

On the other hand, it was hard to believe that someone so gentle could be a monster. What *did* he look like then? Was he as handsome as Psyche imagined? If only she could have a glimpse of him.

As the day went on, the mixture of fear and curiosity became too much for Psyche, and she decided to act on her sisters' advice.

That evening, when she was sure her husband was fast asleep, she lit the lamp that she had hidden beneath the bed, and picked up the long, sharp carving knife.

As the light from the lamp streamed over the sleeping face, Psyche gasped. Far from being a monster, her husband was Love himself. He was Cupid, the most charming and beautiful of all the gods. Psyche recognized the well-known features, the golden hair, and, folded beneath the shoulders,

the soft white wings. At the foot of the bed lay Cupid's famous bow and the quiver of arrows.

Curious about the arrows, Psyche drew one of them out. Then, with trembling fingers, she touched its point. It pierced her flesh, and she was startled. The lamp shook in her hand, spilling scalding oil onto Cupid's shoulder.

Cupid awoke and saw at once what had happened. "Psyche," he said gravely, "I loved you and trusted you, and I thought you, in turn, loved and trusted me. Instead, you thought me a monster. You were ready to cut off my head."

Without another word Cupid went to the casement, spread his wings, and flew into the night.

More deeply in love than ever, Psyche called to him from the window, begging him to return and forgive her.

Cupid paused in his flight and looked down. "Psyche," he said sadly, "out of love for you I disobeyed my mother, Venus. She hates you, you know. She ordered me to make you fall in love with some vile creature. Instead I fell in love with you myself. To keep our love a secret, I never revealed myself, not even to you. But you doubted me, so now we must part. Without trust there can be no love."

Filled with remorse, Psyche lay down and waited for morning. When the sun rose, she found herself in a barren field. The palace and the gardens around it had vanished. She scarcely noticed. Her one thought was to find Cupid. "He no longer loves me," she thought, "and all because I listened to my sisters instead of to my own heart. I doubted Cupid and now he doubts me. I'll find him and somehow prove that I love him—or die in the trying."

Psyche set out at once. Day and night, often with no food or rest, she searched endlessly. No spot was too wild or remote, no mountain too rugged, no forest too dense for her. From one end of the land to the other she wandered, but there was no trace of Cupid anywhere.

After parting with Psyche, Cupid had flown up to Mount Olympus. There, in his mother's palace, he was slowly recovering from the scalding that Psyche had given him. More painful than the scalding was the smart of his disappointment. The love he had shared with Psyche had seemed perfect, but she had doubted him.

Cupid's mother, Venus, was away at the seashore. The palace was empty and filled with echoes. To keep Cupid company, a kindhearted little dove took to perching on his window sill each morning.

It was not long before Cupid was pouring out his heart to the little bird. He told her about Psyche and all about their secret marriage. His voice aquiver with self pity, he said "I gave her my love, yet she doubted me."

The dove always listened patiently. Then one day she gently pointed out, "You complain that Psyche doubted you, but you never fully trusted Psyche, did you? You always remained invisible."

"But if she had known who I was, she might have spoken

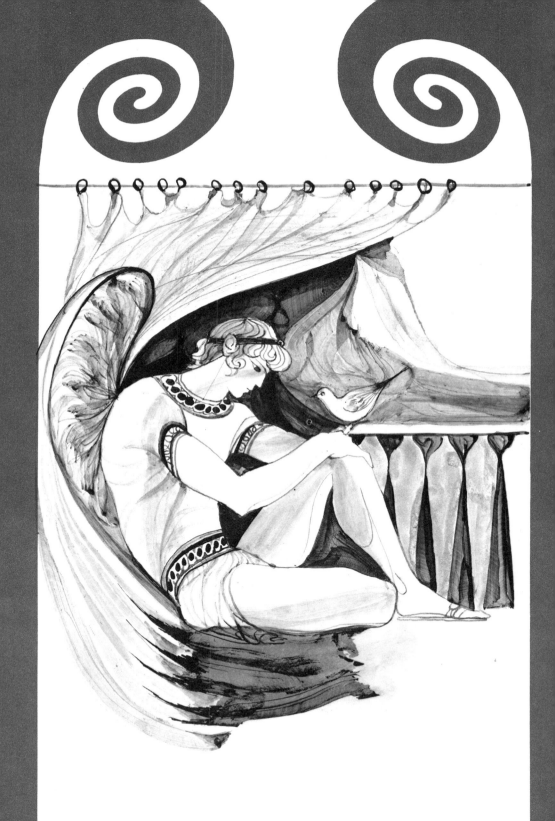

of it," Cupid explained, "and word might have reached my mother's ears."

"Perhaps," murmured the dove. "But where there is no trust there can be no love." With a flutter of wings, the little bird went on her way, leaving Cupid with much to ponder.

"If I had placed in Psyche the same trust that I asked of her, would we be apart like this?" he said to himself. The thought filled him with a deep longing to see Psyche.

In the meantime, a meddlesome sea gull heard that Cupid

was in residence at his mother's home, without her knowledge or permission. Hoping to stir up some trouble, the gull brought the news to Venus as she was bathing in the sea.

"What is more," the gull screamed, "gossip has it that your son has been spending a great deal of time with a certain maiden."

Venus was furious, but she managed to restrain herself. "Tell me," she asked slyly, "do you happen to know the name of the maiden my son finds so alluring? Is she one of the Hours, perhaps, or one of the Muses?"

"Quite the contrary," screamed the sea gull. "The one your son adores is only a mortal. Her name is Psyche."

At the sound of that name, Venus went into a frenzy. Summoning her chariot, she drove at full speed to her palace on Mount Olympus. There, just as the gull had said, was Cupid, stronger now but still pale and wan enough to give almost any mother some concern.

Venus was too beside herself even to notice. "A fine way to show your love and respect!" she scolded Cupid. "I asked you to cause Psyche to fall in love with someone vile. Instead you had the impudence to fall in love with the wretched girl yourself. I promise you that you will regret it!"

"We shall see about that," declared Cupid. Gathering up his bow and arrows, he prepared to leave. His mother's scolding had made his longing for Psyche all the greater.

Aware of her son's intentions, Venus called her servants and had Cupid locked in a room with barred windows.

She herself hurried off to consult her mother-in-law Juno and her aunt Ceres, the gentle harvest goddess. Quickly she told them how Cupid had disobeyed her by falling in love with Psyche. "It is clear that I shall have to destroy her," she finished.

To her annoyance, both goddesses tried to dissuade her. "Was it really so wicked of the boy?" they asked. "If Cupid has a romantic nature, he is only taking after his mother, is he not?"

"Well," sniffed Venus, "I did think I could expect some help or at least a bit of sympathy from two so close to me. It appears that I was mistaken."

Psyche, meanwhile, went on with her search for Cupid. Late one afternoon she was making her way toward the top of a steep mountain when a beautiful temple came into view. Filled with hope, she quickened her pace.

Once again she was disappointed. The temple showed no sign of belonging to Cupid. Scattered carelessly about the floor were corn stalks, sheaves of wheat, ears of barley, sickles, rakes, and other harvest tools.

"I need all the divine help I can get," thought Psyche. And with this in mind she began putting things into the kind of order befitting a god or goddess.

It was the temple of Ceres, the kindly harvest goddess. Touched by Psyche's devotion, Ceres appeared, saying, "How can you take the time to put my temple in order? How can you think of anything but your own safety, child? Don't you know that Venus is searching for you? She plans to destroy you."

"Let me hide here behind the sheaves until her anger cools," begged Psyche.

This Ceres refused to allow. "After all," she explained, "Venus is my niece and good friend. She has a quick temper, to be sure, but she is goodhearted. Go and offer to serve her, Psyche. If you are modest and obedient, she might forgive you. She might even give you and Cupid a mother's blessing."

Knowing that a visit to Venus might mean the end of her, Psyche had little hope, but she thanked the goddess and went on her way.

Before long another beautiful temple came into view. This one was sacred to Juno. The name of the goddess was spelled out in gold on the richly embroidered garments that grateful worshippers had hung on branches in the sacred grove surrounding the temple.

Psyche entered and began to pray for protection from Venus. When Juno at last appeared, her answer was much like that of Ceres. "I'd be happy to help you if I could, but Venus is married to my son Vulcan and this would make things very awkward."

With sinking spirits, Psyche went on her way. If two such powerful goddesses could give her no help, there was only one thing left to do. It might be too late, but she would go and humble herself before Venus.

Finding a temple sacred to the goddess of love, Psyche went inside, fell on her knees, and bowed her head. "Allow me to devote my life to you," she begged of Venus. "Let me live only in order to serve you."

When Venus appeared, it was some time before Psyche dared lift her head. Venus's face was distorted with anger. A deep flush covered the lovely complexion. A frown puckered the beautiful brow. The olive-shaped black eyes were ablaze with hatred.

"So you are Psyche, who thinks herself so beautiful!" Venus gave a scornful laugh. "A plainer girl I have yet to see. Have you come to pay respects to Cupid's mother? Or are you here to ask after Cupid himself? He is still suffering from the scalding you gave him!"

Wincing at the news, Psyche collected herself enough to murmur that she had come here to serve Venus.

"To serve me! Well, if you are as worthless as you are

ugly you won't be of much use, I can tell you that. But, come along. We shall soon find out." Her silken robes flowing gracefully about her shapely figure, Venus swept from the temple.

Filled with foreboding, Psyche followed.

Waiting outside were Venus's chariot and her team of sacred white doves, their rainbow-colored necks in jeweled harnesses.

Venus took her place in the chariot, and ordered Psyche to jump on behind. She murmured to the doves and they were off into the upper air.

It was evening when they arrived at Mount Olympus. Psyche was taken to a small chamber for the night. At dawn the next day Venus led her to a large storehouse. There, mixed together in one enormous mound were the wheat, barley, and millet that the goddess fed to her sacred doves.

"Separate these grains into three piles," Venus ordered Psyche. "And finish the task by evening."

Psyche knew very well that a task like this would take weeks or even months to accomplish. Nonetheless, she set to work sorting the grains. Only when the slant of the sunlight told her that it was noonday did she stop to rest. Before her on the granary floor were three pitiful little piles of grain.

All this time a tiny ant had been looking on. Touched by Psyche's courage, she decided to round up an army of other ants. Column after column of them filed into the granary. Then, grain by grain, they sorted out the enormous pile into three separate piles.

Psyche was astonished and overjoyed.

At twilight, when Venus returned from a drive through

the heavens, she was astonished, too—astonished and angry. Flinging Psyche a crust of bread, she went off muttering, "The wretched girl must have had assistance!"

At dawn the next morning Venus had Psyche brought before her. From the palace window Venus pointed out a grove of cypress trees on the far side of a shining river. "Among those trees," she said, "you will find a flock of sheep with golden fleece. I want a hank of the precious fleece. Don't dare return without it."

Still hoping to win the goddess's favor, Psyche set out at once. At the river's edge she heard a murmuring among the reeds that grew there.

By order of the river god, who hated Venus, the reeds were warning Psyche not to cross the river or enter the grove. The heat of the rising sun enraged the sheep with the golden fleece, they explained. Anyone who ventured among them would be gored to death.

"Be patient," the reeds whispered. "At the end of the afternoon the sheep will be lulled to sleep by the gentle

voice of the river god. Only then can you cross safely. Bits of golden wool will be clinging to the bushes and briars."

Following the reeds' instructions, Psyche completed her task and returned to Venus with an armful of golden fleece.

Venus snatched it from her. "This is clearly not your

own doing," she said. "Someone helped you. You have to prove that you can be useful."

Handing Psyche a tiny box, Venus said, "Take this to the palace of Pluto, King of the Underworld. Give the box to Queen Proserpine and ask her to put a bit of her beauty in it. Tell her that, due to the worry you have caused me, I have lost some of my own beauty. Hurry back, for this evening I plan to attend the Olympic Theatre and I want to look my most beautiful."

Psyche knew better than to trust Venus. She was well aware that, this time, the goddess of love and beauty was sending her to her death. "But could death be any worse than life as I know it now?" Psyche asked herself. "It might be easier. And what choice do I have, in any case? I may as well get it over with." So saying, Psyche climbed to the top of a tall tower.

Seeing her prepared to jump, the tower took pity on her. "Will you give up now, child, after all you have endured?" it asked in a gentle rumble. "If you go to the Underworld by this route, you will never return, you know. Now listen carefully."

The kindly tower told Psyche the way to a certain cave that would lead her to the Underworld.

"Take two coins with you," the tower instructed. "Use one of them to bribe Charon the ferryman to row you across the River Styx."

Then the tower told Psyche how to find the palace of Pluto and Proserpine. "Be sure to take along two pieces of bread soaked in honey water," the tower said. "When you reach the palace, toss one of the sops to Cerberus, the three-headed watchdog. Otherwise, you will never get past him alive."

"Once you are inside, Queen Proserpine will give you a royal welcome. Don't be tempted by it. Instead, seat yourself on the floor and accept nothing but a crust of bread. Then deliver your message."

"On your way back," the voice said, "toss the other sop to Cerberus, and use your other coin to bribe the ferryman again."

"Thank you, thank you!" cried Psyche, eager to be on her way.

"One more thing." The tower's voice turned solemn.

"On your way back to Venus with the box of divine beauty, don't be tempted to open it."

"No, indeed!" declared Psyche, her heart full of hope again.

With no trouble at all Psyche found the cave, and passed through it into the Underworld. There, following the tower's instructions, she made her way to the River Styx.

Through the gloom she could see the outline of Charon's ferryboat. Filled with dead souls, it was moving slowly toward the other bank of the river. There the dead would await the judgment of King Pluto. But for the kindly tower, Psyche might well have been among them. Even now, she must take care.

When Charon returned, she bribed him with one of her coins and was taken across the river. Then, following the tower's directions, she found the dark and forbidding palace of Pluto and Proserpine. Cerberus, the three-headed watchdog was fiercer even than she had expected, and her impulse was to turn and run. But she summoned all her courage, threw him a sop, and passed safely by.

Within the palace she asked for Queen Proserpine and waited patiently. When the queen came, her wintry beauty chilled the vast hall but her manner was cordial. She ordered soft cushions for Psyche to sit on and all sorts of tempting dishes.

Tired and hungry as she was, Psyche remembered to refuse them. Seating herself at Proserpine's feet, she accepted only a crust of bread. Then she took out her tiny box. "My mistress Venus sends you her compliments. She asks that you fill this with a bit of your beauty. Her own is a little faded at present."

"By all means," agreed Proserpine, taking the box from her and leaving the room.

When the queen returned with the box, Psyche thanked her and hurried away, shivering as she went.

Tossing the second sop to the fierce watchdog, and bribing the ferryman with the second coin, she made her way back to the cave by which she had entered the Underworld. Groping her way through this damp passageway, she found herself above ground at last.

After the gloom of the lower regions, the dazzling light

of the living world was so welcome that Psyche stopped for a moment and gave thanks.

All went well until her journey was nearly over. Then, seeing Venus's palace in the distance, Psyche pictured herself presenting the goddess with the box of divine beauty.

Psyche's own beauty had once been called divine. Now, it would be a wonder if she had any left at all. Of course, beauty alone would never win back Cupid's love for her. Still, a touch of divine beauty would do no harm.

Pausing, Psyche drew out the tiny box and fingered it. The warning words of the tower came to mind, but she pushed them aside. If she took just a smidgen of the beauty, what harm could that do? It was not as if she were helping herself to the whole boxful.

With trembling fingers, Psyche pried open the lid of the little box. She found nothing at all inside but a deadly sleep that enwrapped her like a shroud. The breath left her body and she sank soundlessly to the ground.

Luckily for Psyche, the same kindhearted dove who had befriended Cupid happened by at that very moment. As fast

as her wings would take her, the little bird flew up to Cupid's window. Cooing to get his attention, she urged him to go to Psyche's rescue.

Completely recovered now, Cupid was still being punished by Venus. The door of his room was still locked and his window still barred. But, such was the power of his love that he managed to bend back the bars. His wings, strong from their long rest, carried him swiftly to the spot where Psyche lay lifeless, the open box on the path beside her.

With a light touch of one of his arrows, Cupid aroused her. Then, gathering up the deadly sleep, he put it back into the box.

"Psyche, Psyche," he said. "Once again your curiosity

has nearly destroyed you. Don't you know that it is forbidden to learn the secret of the beauty of goddesses? And aren't you as beautiful as a goddess yourself? Return to my mother and complete your task."

"But now that I've found you I don't want to leave you," cried Psyche.

"Nor I you," confessed Cupid. "But do as I ask, and go back to my mother." Then, smiling, he kissed her and said mysteriously, "Leave everything else to me."

The lovers parted. Psyche hurried back to the palace of Venus while Cupid flew to the palace of Jupiter. There, at the feet of the King of Heaven, he told of his love for Psyche. "My mother detests her," he explained. "She wants to destroy her."

Jupiter listened in thoughtful silence. "You have never paid me due respect," he said at last. "And think of the mischief you've performed, Cupid, the havoc you have played with the hearts of mortals and gods, even my own heart. Still—I can't forget how I held you on my knee when you were a little fellow," he added, for Jupiter could be softhearted.

"Yes, my boy," he said finally, "I will help you."

Thereupon, Jupiter called a council of all the gods and goddesses, with heavy fines for those who were absent.

The last to arrive was Venus, her beauty enhanced by the boxful she had borrowed from Queen Proserpine. Well aware of all the heads turning in her direction, she swept proudly down the aisle of the amphitheater. Her eyes widened in surprise when she caught sight of Cupid.

From his throne Jupiter addressed the council, explaining the purpose of the gathering. "It has to do with this young god here." He motioned toward Cupid. "A matter of discipline." Jupiter reminded the council of all the mischief Cupid had performed with his bow and arrows. "He has lived the life of a carefree child long enough. And, indeed, he has come to realize this himself."

Next, Jupiter told the council about the mortal Psyche, and of Cupid's love for her. When he spoke of her great beauty, Venus turned pale with anger.

This was not lost on Jupiter, but he went on to describe Psyche's wanderings and the hardships she had faced, all out of love for Cupid.

"At last," Jupiter declared, "Cupid is convinced that Psyche no longer doubts him but loves him as deeply as he loves her. And, he admits his failure to trust Psyche. He has learned that, where there is no trust, there is no true love."

"Now," the King of the gods concluded, "I propose to join these two together in marriage. Bear in mind that this will keep young Cupid out of mischief. We will all be safer from his dangerous arrows."

The gods and goddesses could be heard murmuring their approval—all but Venus. In her place near the front of the theater, she sat fuming. Had she dared, she would have cried out in loud protest. How could Jupiter approve the marriage of her son to a lowly mortal, and one she hated above all others?

Jupiter read her thoughts, and proceeded to calm her. "Fear not," he said. "This will be a marriage of equals, Venus. I intend to make Psyche immortal. And while she is beautiful, no beauty in heaven or on earth can compare with yours, Venus. Didn't I myself once proclaim this?"

Pleased and flattered, Venus suddenly remembered that

anger could mar her beauty. She calmed herself and began smiling. "Jupiter is so wise," she remarked to the god in the seat beside her.

Mercury was sent to fetch Psyche from Venus's palace where she had been awaiting word of her fate. The council stirred with anticipation. Cupid could not contain himself. Springing from his seat, he fixed his gaze on the entrance.

When Psyche appeared, timid among these bright beings, Cupid sent her a radiant smile. Indeed the gods and goddesses filling the vast theater were all smiling. But, more astonishing than anything else, as Psyche passed down the aisle, Venus caught her hand and whispered her forgiveness.

Then Jupiter held out a goblet of nectar. "Drink, Psyche," he said, "drink and become a goddess."

Psyche drank, and as she did a radiance came to her face and soft white wings appeared at her shoulders.

"Come, Cupid," Jupiter summoned the bridegroom. The King of Heaven himself performed the marriage ceremony.

The wedding breakfast was such as only gods and goddesses know. The ambrosia was more exquisite in flavor

than anything one could imagine. The nectar had been gathered from a thousand different kinds of flowers.

Cupid and Psyche sat in the place of honor. Beside them sat King Jupiter and Queen Juno, then the other gods and goddesses in the order of their importance.

The Hours decorated the palace with red roses.

The Graces sprinkled it with special fragrances.

To the music of flute and pipes, the Muses chanted a joyful wedding hymn.

Then Apollo, the sun god, played his lyre and sang a solo so lovely that Venus stepped forward and began dancing to it. As she danced, she smiled radiantly at Cupid and Psyche.

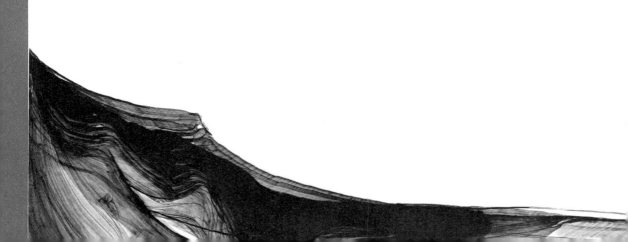

Author's Note

A few pages on Cupid and Psyche appear in my book *Hearts, Cupids, and Red Roses: The Story of the Valentine Symbols*. As I wrote them, an old fondness for this romantic and lovely story was reawakened.

Like myths handed down from ancient times, like Bible stories, or fairy tales deriving from feudal times, the story of Cupid and Psyche must be viewed within its own context, the Greece of nearly two thousand years ago.

First appearing in written form in an allegorical fable by Apuleius, it is said to represent the progress of the human soul toward perfection.

The soul (Psyche), originating in heaven where all is love (Cupid), is condemned for a time to wander the earth, undergoing hardship and misery. If the soul proves worthy, it will in the end return to heaven and be reunited with love, as Psyche is reunited in the story with Cupid.

292
B

Barth, Edna
Cupid and Psyche

83-5354

292
B

Barth, Edna

Cupid and Psyche

83-5354

10.95

DATE	BORROWER'S NAME	
	Kirsten Klint 10-A	
	more	
FEBR		